RISE OF THE GUARDIANS

THE STORY OF JACK FROST

adapted by Farrah McDoogle
illustrated by Larry Navarro

Simon Spotlight
New York London Toronto Sydney New Delhi

SIMON SPOTLIGHT

An imprint of Simon & Schuster Children's Publishing Division

1230 Avenue of the Americas, New York, New York 10020

Rise of the Guardians © 2012 DreamWorks Animation, L.L.C. All rights reserved.

All rights reserved, including the right of reproduction in whole or in part in any form.

SIMON SPOTLIGHT and colophon are registered trademarks of Simon & Schuster, Inc.

For information about special discounts for bulk purchases, please contact Simon & Schuster Special Sales at 1-866-506-1949

or business@simonandschuster.com.

Manufactured in the United States of America 0812 LAK

First Edition 1 2 3 4 5 6 7 8 9 10

ISBN 978-1-4424-5305-0

ISBN 978-1-4424-5306-7 (eBook)

My name is Jack Frost. How do I know that? The moon told me so. But that's all he ever told me.

For a long time I wondered who I was and what I was meant to do. It would take me many years to find out.

This is my story . . .

My story begins with a dark frozen pond and a cold moonlit night. I emerged from the ice, unsure of who I was or why I was there. Then I saw something glinting in the moonlight. It was a staff . . . a magical staff!

I knew that the staff was meant to be mine.

This staff was like a magic wand but even better!
By using it, I could create ice and frost!

"How about some ice with that water?"

I quickly discovered what an awesome power
this was . . . and how much fun I could have with it!

Have you ever had the day off from school for a snow day? Well, that was me! I can *create* snow days!

Jamie needed some help starting a snowball fight. Do you know the best way to start one? It's simple, really . . . just throw a snowball! If you're invisible like me, then no one can tell where it came from and *voilà* . . . instant snowball fight!

The fun ended when Jamie lost his tooth. But he didn't care
because he knew it meant the Tooth Fairy would be coming that night.

I watched and waited with Jamie for Tooth to come, but I wasn't
very happy about it. You see, the Tooth Fairy brings joy to children,
and the children believe in her. But what about *me*? I bring joy to
them with snow days and winter fun, but no one believed in *me*.
And because they didn't believe in me, no one could *see* me.

Later that night I was captured by Yetis and whisked to
the North Pole!

And by whisked, I mean that the Yetis shoved me in a sack, and
I was tossed like a piece of luggage through a magic portal. It wasn't
exactly a pleasant trip, but I was excited to see North's Workshop.
I had tried to break in for years!

I couldn't believe who was waiting for me at North's Palace: North, the big guy himself, Bunny, Tooth, and Sandy. Together they are known as the Guardians of Childhood.

My first words to North were, "You've gotta be kidding me!"
But they weren't kidding!

Why did the Guardians drag me all the way to their big meeting at the North Pole? Well, they wanted *me* to join them!

They told me that the Man in the Moon had chosen me to help protect the children of the world from Pitch . . . who you may know as the Boogeyman.

I told them they were wrong . . . that I wasn't meant to be a Guardian. "You're hard work and deadlines. I'm snowballs and fun times," I told them. In other words . . . thanks, but no thanks.

That's when North took me into his workshop for a private chat. He
showed me a Russian nesting doll. At the center was a tiny baby with
big eyes. He told me that those big eyes represent what's at his center:
his ability to see joy and wonder in everything.

"Who are you, Jack Frost?" he then asked me. "What is your center?"

Before I could answer, Tooth's palace was attacked . . . by Pitch!
All the baby teeth that store children's memories were stolen. It was up
to the Guardians to get the teeth back.

Tooth's Mini Teeth were kidnapped too. There was no way Tooth
could collect the teeth from all the children around the world without
help. If she failed, then the children would stop believing in her.

When I found out that *my* baby teeth—the ones that held *my* memories—were missing, I knew I had to help.

But Pitch had only just begun. He went on to launch a full-out attack against the Guardians. Pitch's Nightmares gave terrible dreams to children, and they stopped believing in the Sandman.

Then Easter was ruined, and children stopped believing in
the Easter Bunny.

And it was my fault. I let Pitch get away because he used my
teeth to distract me.

I almost had him! I'd chased Pitch through his dark tunnels until I caught him. But the lure of my baby teeth—my memories—was too strong.

I found out who I was! I had saved my sister. I was a hero! But just as I figured that out, I worried it might be too late. North was right—the Man in the Moon was never wrong! I *was* brave enough to be a Guardian!

The Guardians were disappointed in me. But I proved to them that I was on their side . . . and that I was meant to be a Guardian.

Together we faced Pitch and his
Nightmares one last time . . . and
together we defeated them!

And that's how I became a Guardian.

I took an oath to guard with my life the hopes, wishes, and dreams of children.

I will always be there to guard and protect *you*.

And the next time you have a snow day . . . think of me and start an awesome snowball fight! Just remember to duck!